Rooney 'Roo

Barbara deRubertis
Illustrated by Eva Vagreti Cockrille

The Kane Press
New York

Cover Design: Sheryl Kagen

Library of Congress Cataloging-in-Publication Data

DeRubertis, Barbara.
Rooney 'Roo/Barbara deRubertis; illustrated by Eva Vagreti Cockrille.
p. cm.
"A let's read together book."

Summary: Rooney 'Roo is a rather solitary kangaroo until he learns to share his love of reading with a friend.
ISBN 1-57565-044-4 (pbk.: alk. paper)
[1. Kangaroos--Fiction. 2. Books and reading--Fiction. 3. Bandicoots--Fiction. 4. Cockatoos--Fiction.
5. Friendship--Fiction. 6. Stories in rhyme.] I. Vagreti Cockrille, Eva, ill. II. Title.
PZ8.3.D455Ro 1998
[E]–dc21 97-44310
CIP
AC

10 9 8 7 6 5 4 3 2

First published in the United States of America in 1998 by The Kane Press.
Printed in Mexico

Look at little
Rooney 'Roo.
He's such a busy
kangaroo.

For Rooney 'Roo
can read! It's true!
He is a *reading*
kangaroo.

Every morning,
Mama 'Roo
says, “Find a friend
to play with you.”

Then Rooney frowns
He has a look
that says, “I'd rather
read a book.”

At noon, his mama calls, "Yoo hoo! Where *is* my little kangaroo?"

She sees that he is by the brook where he is looking at a book.

And when the moon
is in the sky,
Rooney's Mama
says, "Oh, my!

"Put down your book.
It's time for bed.
Put down your book.
Put down your head."

Soon Mama 'Roo
begins to snooze.
Then Rooney grins.
"What shall I choose?

Fairy tales?
History?
Poetry?
Mystery?"

utback
oetry
DINGO JOE
Funny
Fairy
Tales
by A.
Kookaburra
oky
tery
ky Wallaby
HISTORY
OF
AUSTRALIA
by Salty
Crocodile

Healthy BIRDS Are Happy BIRDS
Super Duper Soup

The next day Mama
says, "Today!
Today you must go
out and play!

"The woods are full
of other 'roos.
And bandicoots.
And cockatoos.

"I'm proud that you're
a reading 'roo.
But I'd like you
to make friends, too."

As Rooney hops,
he hears a hoot.
It sounds like Randy
Bandicoot!

Randy's in
a droopy mood.
He's cooked a pot
of goopy food.

"I goofed!" he cries.
"What can I do?
My soup is goop.
Boo hoo! Boo hoo!"

Rooney says,
"I have a book—
a book for cooks!
Let's take a look!

"But first you must
dump out this goop.
Then we can make
a *super* soup."

Rooney reads
the cooking book.
Randy listens
as he cooks.

Soon the food
tastes very good.
Rooney grins,
"I knew it would!

"So when you're in
the mood to cook,
please come and get
my cooking book!"

Now Rooney hops
below the trees.
Then Rooney stops.
He hears a sneeze.

Another sneeze!
"A-choo. A-CHOO!"
It's sneezing Cookie
Cockatoo!

She wipes her eyes.
She blows her nose.
She shivers from
her head to toes.

"Excuse me, please,"
says Rooney 'Roo.
"But I can be
of help to you."

Rooney says,
"I have this book.
It's just for birds.
Let's take a look!"

Cookie coughs. She then swoops down to see what Rooney 'Roo has found.

"I think that you
have got the flu,"
says Rooney 'Roo.
"Here's what to do.

"Drink lots of water
from this pool.
Then cover up,
if you feel cool.

"Get lots of rest
each afternoon.
And you will feel
much better soon."

"Thanks!" says Cookie
Cockatoo.
"Toodle-oo!" says
Rooney 'Roo.

Super
Duber

Rooney scoots.
He zips and zooms.

He bounces, hops,
be-bops, and booms.

Rooney calls to
Mama, "Look!
I made a friend
with each new book!

"It's fun to share
a book! It's true!
I am a *friendly*
reading 'roo!"

ROONEY'ROO'S
LIBRARY
Share a book.
Make a friend!
DINGO JOE
Poetry
CRAFTS
STRAW ANIMALS
70

Now Rooney's friends
come every day.
They read and learn!
They laugh and play!